Get Me OUT of This Book

RULES & TOOLS FOR BEING BRAVE

by **Kalli Dakos** and **Deborah Cholette**

Illustrated by **Sara Infante**

HOLIDAY HOUSE • NEW YORK

For the memory of my wonderful aunt Helen and to my cousin Nick,
who keeps us laughing with funny thoughts, and to the entire Galanos family
—K.D.

To my daughter Samantha Sproule, who has never been afraid to turn the page
—D.C.

To the Navy SEALs, who inspired us with their strategies for
overcoming challenging missions
—K.D. & D.C.

To my sister Marta who, when I was afraid, always said to me:
Calm, Courage and Confidence
—S.I.

THE SCARIEST BOOK EVER

ADVENTURES UNDERGROUND

Bedtime Stories

AT THE SEA

I'm Max. I'm a bookmark who used to be **SCARED TO DEATH** of books. The pictures **FREAKED** me out!

When I was put on a page with a king cobra, I couldn't
LOOK and I SHOOK and I SCREAMED—

GET ME OUT OF THIS BOOK!

The Jungle Book

But no one heard, and I was trapped!

PLAN
ahead
&
PLAN
ahead

think good thoughts

1

BREATHE

That's when I snapped and went back to school for a
Special Bookmark Badge. I had to learn how to handle
the **SCARIEST** pictures in the **SCARIEST** books.

My trainer was tough. He taught me
RULES AND TOOLS for looking right
at SCARY.

Then he put me in a book on a page with a SHARK.
It had giant white teeth, and it was swimming toward
my face. I could almost feel the bites, and my heart went
BA-BOOM! BA-BOOM! **BA-BOOM!**

I couldn't LOOK and I SHOOK and I SCREAMED—

GET Me OUT OF this BOOK!

And then I remembered Number One of the **RULES AND TOOLS.**

Breathe Deeply

Deep breath in,

deep breath out.

Deep breath in,

deep breath out.

I kept breathing and breathing and breathing and
breathing until my heart slowed down to *ba-boom*,
ba-boom, *ba-boom*, and I could look past the teeth
to the eyes of the shark and say, "You're just a picture,
and you can't hurt me!"

CREEPY was next.

When I was put on a page with hundreds of
cockroaches crawling toward me like an army,
I couldn't LOOK and I SHOOK and I SCREAMED—

And then I remembered Number Two of the
RULES AND TOOLS.

Make a Plan

I decided to think up a song and
to sing really loudly.

Macaroni,
Macaroni,
One,
Two,
Three.
You're not real,
And you can't hurt me.

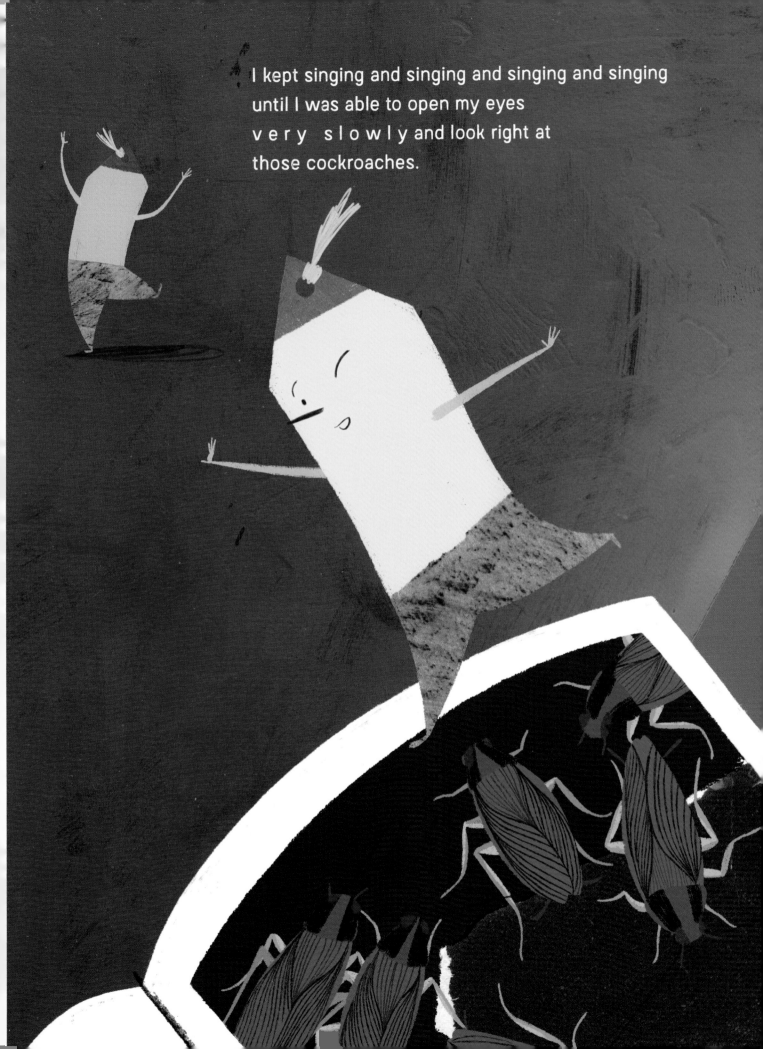

I kept singing and singing and singing and singing
until I was able to open my eyes
v e r y   s l o w l y and look right at
those cockroaches.

The next book was HAUNTED!

I was put on a page that was darker than dark,
and I knew spooky dead things were hiding there.
I couldn't LOOK and I SHOOK and I
SCREAMED—

GET ME OUT OF THIS BOOK!

And then I remembered Number Three of the
RULES AND TOOLS.

Think Good Thoughts

"I will get through this dark page," I said to myself. "If other bookmarks can do it, I can, too!"

I couldn't see anything at
all, so I decided to practice.
What would I do if a ten-foot
skeleton came out of the dark
and was ready to attack me?

I'd **PUNCH** him! Then I'd watch his bones fall apart into a pile on the ground. They would look so silly that I'd start laughing and laughing and laughing and laughing.

When I stopped practicing I was still all alone
in the dark, but I realized that the good thoughts
were right there to help me.

I graduated from Bookmark School, and I loved
my Special Bookmark Badge.

I had learned RULES AND TOOLS, and now I
WANTED to go into the SCARIEST pictures in
the SCARIEST books.

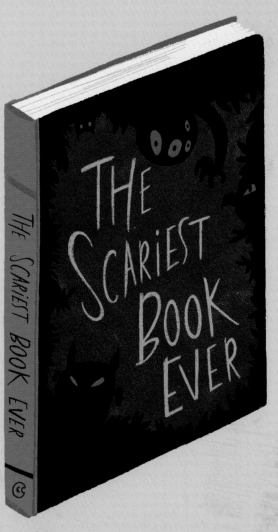

THE SCARIEST BOOK EVER

Before long, I found myself in a closet . . . a dark closet . . . a locked closet. . . . I was trapped inside with a monster that had *seven hairy heads*! I wanted to **freak out.**

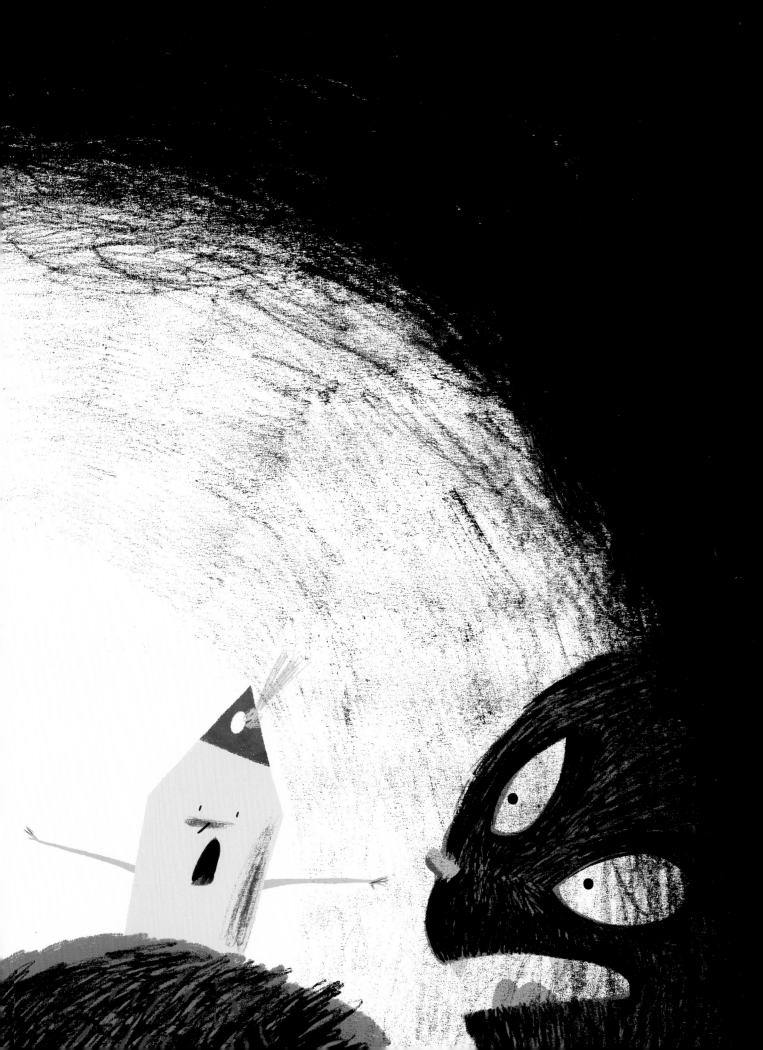

But I remembered that I had **RULES AND TOOLS**, and I knew what to do.

I started to breathe deeply—deep breath in, deep breath out—until I was feeling calm.

I made a plan—I stood up very tall and pretended
I was not afraid.

I thought good thoughts—I could do this! I could
handle this! I would be all right.

I looked right at
the fourteen eyes
in the seven heads.

One head was looking up.

One head was looking down.

One head was looking halfway around.

One head was screaming.
One head was trembling.
One head was closing its eyes.
And one head was sobbing big gooey tears.

And that's when I realized that the big hairy monster with all those heads was afraid of the dark closet, too. I yelled at the heads, "Don't be afraid! Tomorrow someone will turn the page in the book, and you'll get out, and everything will be okay!"

And then I knew that I would be okay, too, even in the SCARIEST pictures in the SCARIEST books because the RULES AND TOOLS really work!

AUTHORS' NOTE

After many rewrites of *Get Me Out of This Book*, there was a consistent theme that Max was afraid of the scary pictures in books. Deborah thought he should go to Bookmark School to learn how to deal with his fears. Kalli was a big fan of the Navy SEALs and their training methods. The authors had Max use three Navy SEALs strategies to overcome fearful situations:

Breathe Deeply

Make a Plan

Think Good Thoughts

Text copyright © 2019 by Kalli Dakos and Deborah Cholette
Illustrations copyright © 2019 by Sara Infante
All Rights Reserved
HOLIDAY HOUSE is registered in the U.S. Patent and Trademark Office.
Printed and bound in October 2018 at Tien Wah Press, Johor Bahru, Johor, Malaysia.
The artwork was created with mixed media.
www.holidayhouse.com
First Edition
1 3 5 7 9 10 8 6 4 2
Library of Congress Cataloging-in-Publication Data
Names: Dakos, Kalli, author. | Cholette, Deborah, author. | Infante, Sara, illustrator.
Title: Get me out of this book: rules and tools for being brave / by Kalli Dakos and Deborah Cholette;
illustrated by Sara Infante. | Description: First edition. | New York : Holiday House, [2019]
Summary: Max, a skittish bookmark, learns to conquer his fear of books by using
rules and tools inspired by the Navy SEALs.
Identifiers: LCCN 2017055733 | ISBN 9780823438624 (hardcover)
Subjects: | CYAC: Fear—Fiction. | Self-help techniques—Fiction.
Bookmarks—Fiction. | Books and reading—Fiction.
Classification: LCC PZ7.D15223 Get 2019
DDC [E]—dc23 LC record available at https://lccn.loc.gov/2017055733